How Koala Got a Stumpy Tail

by Jackie Walter and Yekyung Kwon

Long ago, Koala and Tree Kangaroo
were very good friends.
Both of them had very long tails.
They jumped from tree to tree,
using their tails to help them.

One year, there was no rain.

The rivers and streams dried up.

There was no water to drink.

The trees began to die.

"We will die without water,"
cried Koala. "What can we do?"

Tree Kangaroo had an idea.

He told Koala about his mother.

She had found water when

there was no rain.

"She dug a hole at the bottom of a dried-up stream. She dug for hours and hours. At last, water filled the hole."

"We can do that!" cried Koala.

They set off to find

a dried-up stream.

After a long, hot walk,

they found one.

"We can dig here,"
said Tree Kangaroo.
"Okay," said Koala. "But I will need
a rest before I can dig."

Koala climbed up a tall tree to rest.

Tree Kangaroo began to dig.

After a while, he called out to Koala,

"Hey, Koala, come and help me dig!"

Koala started to climb down
from the tree. "Ouch!" he cried.
"I've got a thorn in my paw!
I cannot dig with a sore paw."
So, Koala stayed in the tree.

Tree Kangaroo kept on digging. After a while, he called out, "Hey, Koala, I'm getting tired and thirsty. It must be your turn to dig."

Koala started to climb down.

"Oh no. I feel dizzy," he called.

"I need more rest."

Tree Kangaroo was angry,

but he kept on digging.

And at last, water came up

into the hole.

"Water!" cried Tree Kangaroo.

16

Koala jumped down from the tree.
He pushed Tree Kangaroo out of
the way. He stuck his head
into the hole and began to drink
the water. He drank and drank.

Tree Kangaroo was angry.

"Leave some for me!" he cried.

But Koala kept on drinking.

So, Tree Kangaroo grabbed Koala's

long tail and started to pull him out

of the hole.

He pulled so hard that Koala's tail broke clean off!

And that is how Koala got a stumpy tail.

Franklin Watts
First published in Great Britain in 2022
by Hodder and Stoughton
Copyright © Hodder and Stoughton Ltd, 2022

Series Editors: Jackie Hamley and Melanie Palmer
Development Editors and Series Advisors: Dr Sue Bodman and Glen Franklin
Series Designer: Peter Scoulding and Cathryn Gilbert

A CIP catalogue record for this book is
available from the British Library.

ISBN 978 1 4451 8390 9 (hbk)
ISBN 978 1 4451 8391 6 (pbk)
ISBN 978 1 4451 8452 4 (library ebook)
ISBN 978 1 4451 8451 7 (ebook)

Printed in China

Franklin Watts
An imprint of
Hachette Children's Group
Part of Hodder and Stoughton
Carmelite House
50 Victoria Embankment
London EC4Y 0DZ

An Hachette UK Company
www.hachette.co.uk

www.reading-champion.co.uk

FSC
www.fsc.org
MIX
Paper from
responsible sources
FSC® C104740

Answer to Story order: 4, 5, 1, 3, 2